WALT DISNEY'S
Cinderella

Story adapted by Jane Werner
Illustrated by Retta Scott Worcester

Digital scanning and restoration services provided by
Tim Lewis of Disney Publishing Worldwide and Ron Stark of S/R Labs

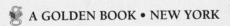

A GOLDEN BOOK • NEW YORK

www.randomhouse.com/kids/disney
www.goldenbooks.com
ISBN: 0-7364-2151-3
Printed in the United States of America
First Random House Edition   10

nce upon a time, there lived a kindly gentleman. He had a fine home and a lovely daughter, and he gave her all that money could buy—a pony, a puppy named Bruno, and many beautiful dresses.

But the little girl wished for a mother and for other children to play with. So her father married a woman with two daughters of her own. Now, he thought, his daughter had everything to make her happy.

But alas! The kindly gentleman soon died. And his
second wife was harsh and cold to her lovely stepdaughter.
She cared only for her two ugly daughters.

Everyone called the stepdaughter Cinderella now since
she sat by the cinders to keep warm as she worked hard,
dressed only in rags.

But Cinderella was not sad. She made friends with the birds who flew to her windowsill. And her best friends of all were—guess who—the mice!

The mice lived in the attic with Cinderella. She made little clothes for them and gave them all names. And they thought Cinderella was the sweetest girl in the world.

Every morning, Cinderella woke from her dreams and went right to work. Out back she set a bowl of milk for the Stepmother's disagreeable cat, who watched for his chance to catch the mice. She fed grain to the chickens and ducks and geese. And Cinderella gave some grain to the mice—when they were out of reach of the cat, of course. Then back into the house she went.

Up the long stairway she carried breakfast trays for her Stepmother and her two lazy stepsisters. And down she came with a basket of mending, some clothes to wash, and a long list of jobs to do for the day.

"Now let me see," her Stepmother would say. "You can clean the large carpet in the main hall. And wash all the windows, upstairs and down. Scrub the terrace. Sweep the stairs—and then you may rest."

Now, across the town was the palace of the King. And one day the King himself was giving orders to the Great Grand Duke. "The Prince must marry!" said the King. "It is high time!"

"But first he must fall in love," said the Duke.

"We can arrange that," said the King. "We shall give a great ball this very night and invite every girl in the land!"

There was much excitement when the invitation to the King's ball came.

"How delightful!" the stepsisters said. "We are going to the palace to a ball!"

"And I," said Cinderella, "I am invited, too!"

"Yes, you!" mocked the Stepmother. "Of course you may go, *if* you finish your work," she said. "And *if* you have something suitable to wear. I said *if*."

Cinderella worked all day long. She did not have a
moment to fix herself up, or to give thought to a dress.
"Why, Cinderella, you are not ready," said her
Stepmother when the coach was at the door. "What a shame!"

Poor Cinderella!

But when she got to her room, she saw that her little friends had not forgotten her. They had been gathering discarded items from the stepsisters' rooms to fix a party dress for her.

"Oh, how lovely!" she cried. She looked out the window. The coach was still there. So she started to dress for the ball.

"Wait!" cried Cinderella. "I am coming, too!"

The Stepmother and her daughters all turned at the sound of Cinderella's voice.

"My beads!" cried one stepsister.

"And my ribbon!" cried the other. "And those bows! You thief! Those are mine!"

So they ripped and they tore at the dress until Cinderella was in rags once more. And then they pranced off to the ball.

Poor Cinderella! She ran to the garden and wept as if her heart would break.

But soon she felt someone beside her. She looked up, and through her tears she saw a sweet-faced little woman. "Oh," said Cinderella. "Good evening. Who are you?"

"I am your Fairy Godmother," said the woman. "Now dry your tears. You can't go to the ball looking like that!"

"Let's see now, the first thing you will need is—a pumpkin!" the Fairy Godmother said.

Cinderella was confused, but she brought over a pumpkin.

The Fairy Godmother said some magic words.

Slowly, the pumpkin turned into a fancy coach.

"What we need next are some fine, big—mice!"

At the touch of the wand Cinderella's little friends turned into handsome horses.

Then the old horse became a fine coachman.

And Bruno the dog turned into a footman.

"There," said the Fairy Godmother. "Now hop in, child. The magic only lasts till midnight!"

"But my dress—" Cinderella looked at her rags.

"Of course you can't go in that!" laughed the Fairy Godmother.

The wand waved again, and there stood Cinderella—in the most beautiful gown in the world, and tiny slippers of glass.

The Prince's ball was under way. As soon as Cinderella
appeared in the doorway, the Prince walked over and asked
her to dance.

The King motioned to the musicians, and they struck
up a dreamy waltz. The Prince and Cinderella swirled across
the dance floor. And the King went happily off to bed.

The Prince and Cinderella danced every dance until the clock in the palace tower began to strike midnight. *Bong! Bong!*

"Oh!" cried Cinderella. The magic was about to end!

Without a word she ran out the door. One of her little glass slippers fell off, but she could not stop.

She leaped into her coach and raced for home. But the spell was soon broken.

"Glass slipper!" the mice cried. "Glass slipper!"

Cinderella looked down. Sure enough, there was a glass slipper on the pavement.

"Oh, thank you, Godmother!" she said.

The next morning, the King learned that the Prince wanted to marry the slipper's owner.

"Find her! Scour the kingdom, but find that girl!" he shouted to the Duke.

News of the Duke's search ran on ahead, and the Stepmother dressed her ugly daughters, hoping that one of them would be the Prince's bride.

"The Prince's bride!" whispered Cinderella. "I must dress, too. The Duke must not find me like this."

Cinderella went off to her room, humming a waltzing tune. Then the Stepmother suspected the truth—that Cinderella was the girl the Prince was seeking. So the Stepmother locked her in her room!

"Please let me out—oh, please!" Cinderella cried. But the wicked Stepmother only laughed and went away.

"We will save you!" said the loyal mice. "We will somehow get that key!"

The household was in a flurry. The Grand Duke and his servant had arrived with the glass slipper.

Each stepsister tried to force her foot into the tiny glass slipper. But they failed.

Meanwhile, the mice made themselves into a long, live chain. The mouse at the end dropped down into the Stepmother's pocket. He popped up again with the key to Cinderella's room!

The Grand Duke was about to leave when Cinderella came flying down the stairs.

"Oh, wait, wait, please!" she called. "May I try the slipper on?"

"Of course," said the Duke. But the wicked Stepmother tripped the servant with the slipper. *Crash!* It splintered into a thousand pieces.

"Never mind," said Cinderella. "I have the other here." And she pulled from her pocket the other glass slipper!

Soon she was Princess of the land. And she and her husband, the charming Prince, rode to their palace in a golden coach to live happily ever after!